ED AND THE RIVER OF THE DAMNED

Andrew Fusek Peters
& Stephen Player

Hodder
Children's
Books

Critical acclaim for **Ed and the Witchblood,**
the first book in the Wild Edric Trilogy:

A strong story mixing gruesome fantasy with
contemporary sex, violence and teenage angst. ....
Every image is vividly drawn in a masculine style
with strong characterisation and lots of unusual
perspectives. ... A far more challenging, haunting
and poetic read than its highly illustrated format
might suggest.

— Northern Echo

An uncompromising and unusual story that combines
the contemporary with the historical, aims for the
disaffected jugular. ... In a dramatic climax the two
worlds collide ... Wooing youngsters most comfortable
with strong visual imagery and narrative in film,
TV and computer technology.

— Education Guardian

Brave ... The characters are rather lyrically drawn
(reflecting the strong use of poetry throughout
the book).

— School Librarian

The plot is fast-paced and the black and white
illustrations are great.

— SFX

Dedications:

For Dave Cresswell – S.P.

To all my friends in the Firm –
it really does get better, one day
at a time. – A.F.P.

Hail the sky's long lost daughter,
Air, earth, fire, water;
Life dies, a ghost gives birth,
Water, air, fire, earth;
I stamp and breathe a roaring choir,
Earth, air, water, fire:
Thread of the witch is woven with care,
Fire, earth, water, air;
Bind these elements one by one,
Adding time 'til times are done,
But the sixth, the final prize?
How to meet the enemy's eyes?
Stronger than the singing sword,
This shall have them overawed.

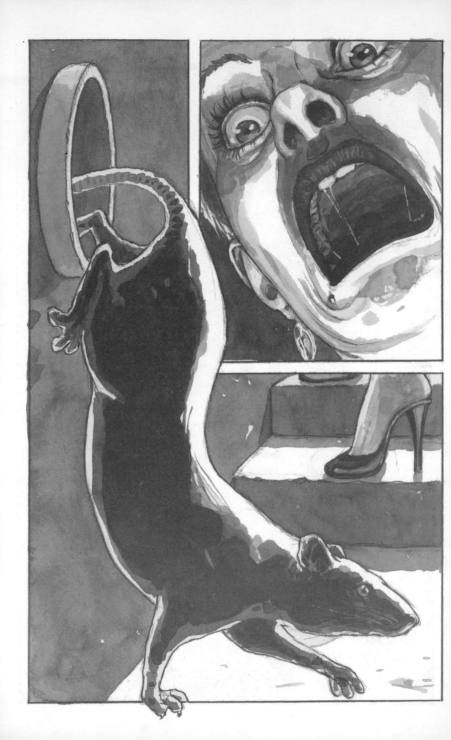

Don't worry Luci, you get all sorts down in that basement. The damp from the old River Fleet attracts them.

VERMIN! Having you to stay in this house is bad enough!

Serves her right. She's a rat-faced excuse for a stepmum. Seems to have forgotten I used to live here.

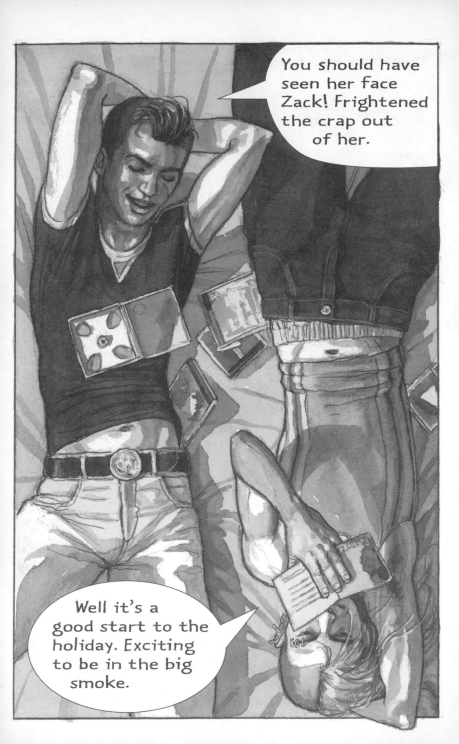

You overdid it there, mate.

But it was beautiful. Everyone. Fantastic. Ed, I love you. You're my best, bestest mate.

And Nat, he's brilliant. Class. Invited us over. Got to go.

No! Got to go home, Zack. You are totally off your trolley!

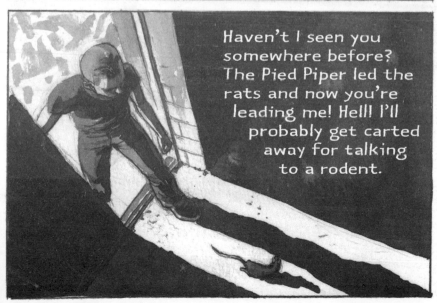

Haven't I seen you somewhere before? The Pied Piper led the rats and now you're leading me! Hell! I'll probably get carted away for talking to a rodent.

Blimey, where did they find this one?

King William Street?
Never seen that on
a tube map.

Not too sure
about this.

Gift of the river, Edric the Wild. Food is nourishment and this little purrer had no more need of its body.

Is that you talking?

No, I am thinking, and you are thoughtful. Listen well.

There was a river here, long ago. Rising in Hampstead, falling through the lush fields of Kings Cross, St Pancras, and turning the mills of old London to work its way to Mother Thames.

When they cut the forest, we moved to the leaning alleyways. The river fed us old guts from the leather-tanners, the odd bloated drunk, dead dogs drowned, dead meat.

When they buried the river and filled it with their sewage, we went deep under the earth. The sewer workers knew us as ghosts, naming us the Milk-Whites.

When they died, silver pennies were placed on their eyes to ward us off. It was said that we were the souls of those who have gone before.

But that was long ago. Later,
metal worms came, digging to find
us, cars carpeted the hills of the
city, but still we are here.

Now, danger. Something is rotten.
There is a strong one, poisoning
heart and soul with potions and
powders. Help us.

And your mother, Edric, is alive and well. She misses you.

My mother! You know her? Where the hell is she? Uh, let me guess – you're not about to tell me, huh? She was always close to animals. My Grandad reckoned she could almost talk with them.

That is your inheritance **and** here is her word. Farewell.

NATURAL HISTORY MUS

Edric the Wild, my only son! I am with you and always with you. Trust the animals more than the humans, especially those close to you. You will see me again, I promise. But I am gathering my strength. Our time will come. Now, you must find the dead end of the river and smash it for the good.

This is too much...

Tastes delicious Luci! You do look after me.

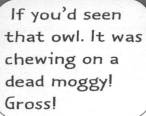

If you'd seen that owl. It was chewing on a dead moggy! Gross!

Chill out mate. It was naked witches last time. Somehow, your corpse-chomping owls are not quite so sexy. Anyhow, good night ahead.

See ya, Shem.

Well, at least this lot are keeping us in business. You see, Nat, it's all about supply and demand. If the youth of today demand to get out of their heads, who are we to deny them the pleasure?

You're not crawling to me, are you? I can't stand crawling things.

No, honestly, not at all.

Well put, boss.

Just remember, dopehead, the big delivery is the day after tomorrow. You need to be at the workshop at 11.30 pronto.

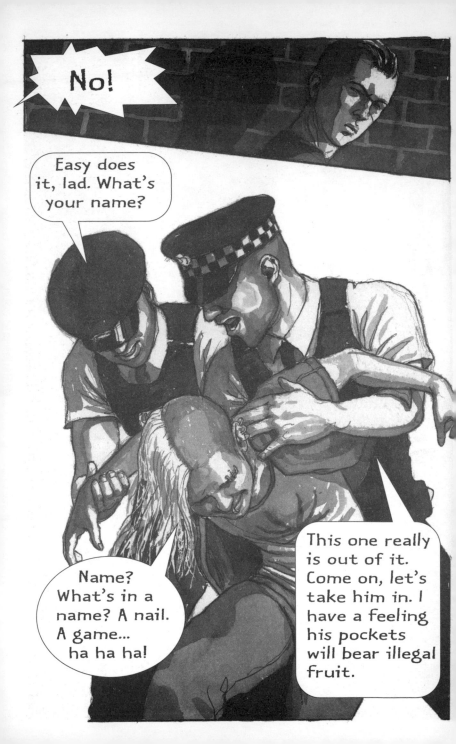

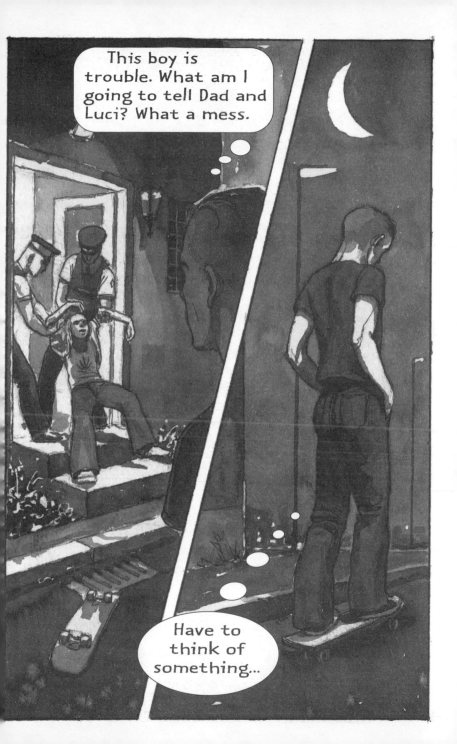

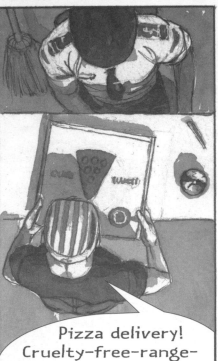

Right Ed, you are in the middle of a police station in broad daylight looking for your mate who has been arrested.

This is not looking good at all.

Owl get there eventually!

KAZ. D. STONE

Very clever Zack — always thought you were a bit backwards. I'm surprised they didn't get the joke.

I'm Ed.

We's wedded to the dark. Got eyes like them rats — searching for that gleam of gold. Your young friend here looks like 'e could do wiv flushin' out. Too much flotsam and jetsam in his mind. By the way, the name's Jim, Jim the Tosher.

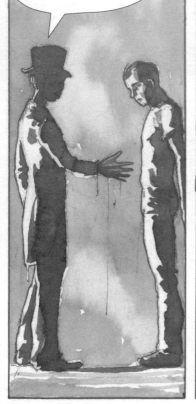

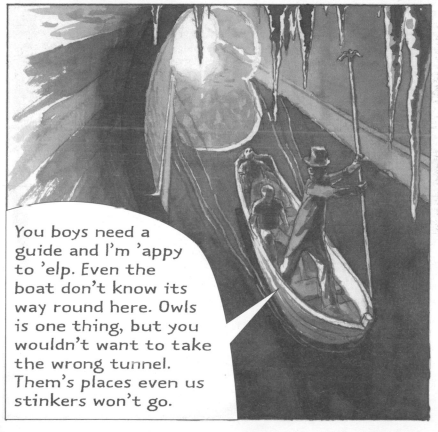

What's the point in going for the guy who supplied the drugs? It's Zach who took them. It's just not that simple.

Good day, Edric. Just call for Jim if you'll be needing me.

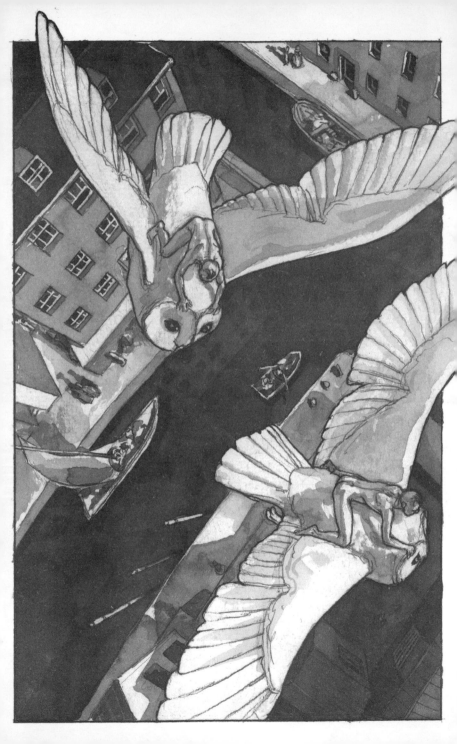

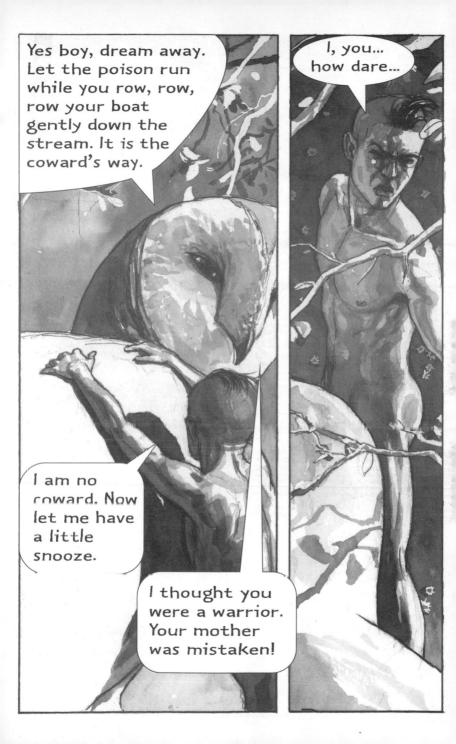

Shem didn't bargain on me when he messed up my best mate's head. If I've got my timing right, Zack's so-called 'friend' should show me the way.

Talk about the devil, or should I say the devil's accomplice, there's the Un-Natural Nal, rushing to meet his 11.30 deadline. Let's find out a bit more about his 'business' partner.

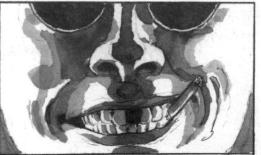

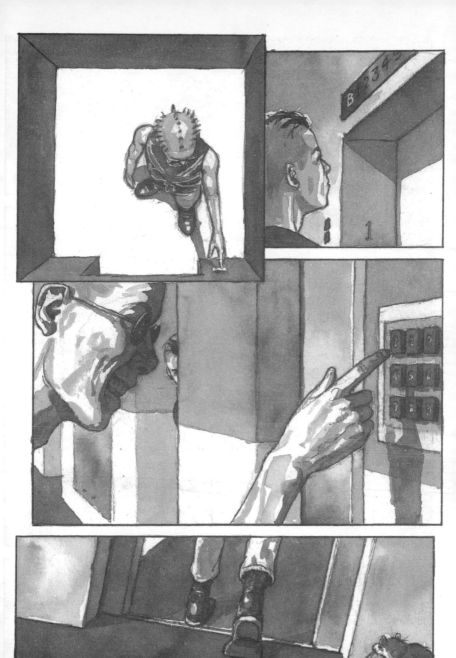

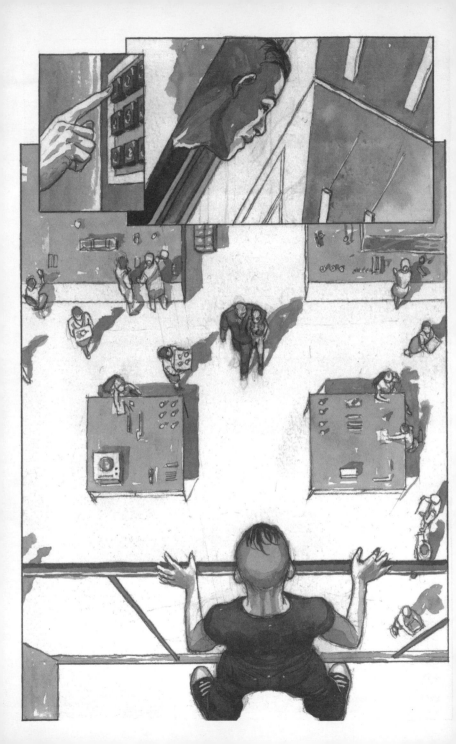

Does the trick quite nicely...

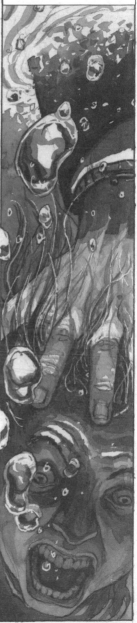

I catch the ones who slip through the cracks of the city. Grateful for a meal and a bed. No-one to miss 'em. Once in a while, one or two tries to face me out. So I pin a picture of them face down in the river on the canteen noticeboard.

Just deal with him, right.

Deal with who, Luci?

Oh, you know. Suppliers.

Oh yeah?

There's tea in the oven for you. You should get home now.

Don't know what that is anymore. Mum vanishes and you conveniently take her place. It's all a bit too easy.

But that's the point, Ed darling. Your adolescent tantrums drove her to distraction!

Dad, it's great being here this holiday, but this house is all wrong without Mum. You never talk about her. Don't you even miss her?

Well, yes, more than you know, son. I've got Luci now, but it's not the same, is it?

No Luci isn't. But I don't think you've sussed that yet. I miss living with you. What if I told you that Mum...

What?

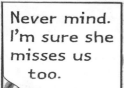
Never mind. I'm sure she misses us too.

Well, when she wrote that letter to us, it seemed a pretty firm goodbye.

Yeah, maybe.

Yeah, yeah. Okay. Night then, Dad. I'm shattered.

And we've been through all that stuff about you living with Grandad for a while till things settle down.

Cooeeeeh there! Mr Pathetic-Gangster-Low-Down-Pimp-Dealer-Man! Remember me?

I'm afraid that seeing my face has brought you a little snooze on the river bed, Sonny!

Oh yeah? Really? Try it!

After him!

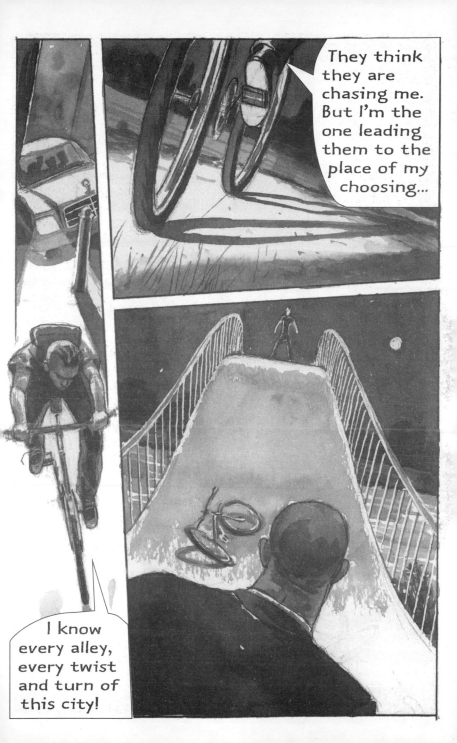

Meanwhile

Woah, that was some trip... But I seem to feel better... Er, hang on, what the hell are you?

'Tis a pleasure to be meeting you. Jim The Tosher – where there's muck, there might be gold... Any friend of Edric the Wild is a friend of mine. Come, we are in haste!

I owe you one there mate! I think I'm a bit sick of the city.

White owls, talking rats, underground rivers, strange dead men in frock coats... some trip. Let's head for the hills.

Hail the sky's long lost daughter,
Air, earth, fire, water;
Life dies, a ghost gives birth,
Water, air, fire, earth;
I stamp and breathe a roaring choir,
Earth, air, water, fire:

Thread of the witch is
woven with care,
Fire, earth, water, air;
Bind these elements one by one,
Adding time 'til times are done,
But the sixth, the final prize?
How to meet the enemy's eyes?
Stronger than the singing sword,
This shall have them overawed.

About the Author and Illustrator

Andrew Fusek Peters has written and edited over forty critically acclaimed books for young people, many with his wife Polly Peters. Together, they wrote the best-selling **Poems With Attitude** and its successor **Poems With Attitude: Uncensored.**

The Guardian said of **Poems With Attitude**:
'Bursting with the raw emotion and hormone-fuelled experimentation of youth. It is rare and welcome to find a collection that speaks so directly to teenagers.'

For more information about Andrew, visit his web site at www.tallpoet.com

Stephen Player is a highly experienced illustrator whose work includes illustrations for books by Clive Barker and Terry Pratchett as well as numerous children's books.
Born in Hertfordshire, he recently moved from London to San Francisco. For more information visit his web site at www.playergallery.com

Also by Andrew Fusek Peters and Stephen Player:

ED AND THE
WITCHBLOOD

Ed's life is hell: an absent mother, a strange town, an old man's sick stories, and Mitch, a violent thug bent on doing him serious harm. But ancient legends never really die and there is something undead waiting under the stone circle on the hill; something about to turn everyone's world upside down.

Gritty and twisted, this powerful tale is as gripping and stylish as any by Stephen King or James Herbert.

"Fast-paced and the ... illustrations are great." - SFX

"[This] uncompromising and unusual story that combines the contemporary with the historical, aims for the disaffected jugular." - Guardian Education

PB 0340865571

Also by Andrew Fusek Peters and Polly Peters:

CRASH

Too young. Too fast. Love and Death. It happens.

It just happens.

Nat: lead singer in a local band, best mates with
Carl: they hang out being lads until
Kate: sees Nat and together, things change.

Going out, getting on, living, loving, arguing, all the normal
stuff really. But all it takes is one moment, a few slow seconds
and nothing will ever be the same again.

Different poetic voices piece together a powerful drama in
which the best and the worst happens. It just happens. The
twists are bitter and the only hope is hope itself.

HB 0340884681
PB 034088469X